THE CAT IN THE HAT

By Dr. Seuss

2 4 6 8 10 9 7 5 3 1

ISBN 0-00-724791-5
ISBN-13 978-0-00-724791-2

© 1957, 1985 by Dr. Seuss Enterprises, L.P.
All Rights Reserved
A Beginner Book published by arrangement with
Random House Inc., New York, USA
First published in the UK 1958
This edition published in the UK 2007 by
HarperCollins*Children's Books,*
a division of HarperCollins*Publishers* Ltd
77-85 Fulham Palace Road
London W6 8JB

Visit our website:
www.harpercollinschildrensbooks.co.uk

Printed and bound in Hong Kong

The sun did not shine.
It was too wet to play.
So we sat in the house
All that cold, cold, wet day.

1

I sat there with Sally.

We sat there, we two.

And I said, "How I wish

We had something to do!"

Too wet to go out

And too cold to play ball.

So we sat in the house.

We did nothing at all.

2

So all we could do was to

Sit!

   Sit!

      Sit!

         Sit!

And we did not like it.

Not one little bit.

And then

Something went BUMP!

How that bump made us jump!

We looked!

Then we saw him step in on the mat!

We looked!

And we saw him!

The Cat in the Hat!

And he said to us,

"Why do you sit there like that?"

"I know it is wet

And the sun is not sunny.

But we can have

Lots of good fun that is funny!"

"I know some good games we could play,"
Said the cat.
"I know some new tricks,"
Said the Cat in the Hat.
"A lot of good tricks.
I will show them to you.
Your mother
Will not mind at all if I do."

Then Sally and I
Did not know what to say.
Our mother was out of the house
For the day.

But our fish said, "No! No!

Make that cat go away!

Tell that Cat in the Hat

You do NOT want to play.

He should not be here.

He should not be about.

He should not be here

When your mother is out!"

"Now! Now! Have no fear.
Have no fear!" said the cat.
"My tricks are not bad,"
Said the Cat in the Hat.
"Why, we can have
Lots of good fun, if you wish,
With a game that I call
Up-up-up with a fish!"

12

"Put me down!" said the fish.

"This is no fun at all!

Put me down!" said the fish.

"I do NOT wish to fall!"

13

"Have no fear!" said the cat.

"I will not let you fall.

I will hold you up high

As I stand on a ball.

With a book on one hand!

And a cup on my hat!

But that is not ALL I can do!"

Said the cat . . .

14

"Look at me!

Look at me now!" said the cat.

"With a cup and a cake

On the top of my hat!

I can hold up TWO books!

I can hold up the fish!

And a little toy ship!

And some milk on a dish!

And look!

I can hop up and down on the ball!

But that is not all!

Oh, no.

That is not all . . .

16

"Look at me!

Look at me!

Look at me NOW!

It is fun to have fun

But you have to know how.

I can hold up the cup

And the milk and the cake!

I can hold up these books!

And the fish on a rake!

I can hold the toy ship

And a little toy man!

And look! With my tail

I can hold a red fan!

I can fan with the fan

As I hop on the ball!

But that is not all.

Oh, no.

That is not all. . . ."

That is what the cat said . . .
Then he fell on his head!
He came down with a bump
From up there on the ball.
And Sally and I,
We saw ALL the things fall!

21

And our fish came down, too.

He fell into a pot!

He said, "Do I like this?

Oh, no! I do not.

This is not a good game,"

Said our fish as he lit.

"No, I do not like it,

Not one little bit!"

22

"Now look what you did!"

Said the fish to the cat.

"Now look at this house!

Look at this! Look at that!

You sank our toy ship,

Sank it deep in the cake.

You shook up our house

And you bent our new rake

You SHOULD NOT be here

When our mother is not.

You get out of this house!"

Said the fish in the pot.

25

"But I like to be here.

Oh, I like it a lot!"

Said the Cat in the Hat

To the fish in the pot.

"I will NOT go away.

I do NOT wish to go!

And so," said the Cat in the Hat,

"So

    so

      so . . .

I will show you

Another good game that I know!"

And then he ran out.

And, then, fast as a fox,

The Cat in the Hat

Came back in with a box.

A big red wood box.

It was shut with a hook.

"Now look at this trick,"

Said the cat.

"Take a look!"

Then he got up on top

With a tip of his hat.

"I call this game FUN-IN-A-BOX,"

Said the cat.

"In this box are two things

I will show to you now.

You will like these two things,"

Said the cat with a bow.

"I will pick up the hook.

You will see something new.

Two things. And I call them

Thing One and Thing Two.

These Things will not bite you.

They want to have fun."

Then, out of the box

Came Thing Two and Thing One!

And they ran to us fast.

They said, "How do you do?

Would you like to shake hands

With Thing One and Thing Two?"

33

And Sally and I

Did not know what to do.

So we had to shake hands

With Thing One and Thing Two.

We shook their two hands.

But our fish said, "No! No!

Those Things should not be

In this house! Make them go!

"They should not be here
When your mother is not!
Put them out!   Put them out!"
Said the fish in the pot.

35

"Have no fear, little fish,"
Said the Cat in the Hat.
"These Things are good Things."
And he gave them a pat.
"They are tame.   Oh, so tame!
They have come here to play.
They will give you some fun
On this wet, wet, wet day."

"Now, here is a game that they like,"
Said the cat.
"They like to fly kites,"
Said the Cat in the Hat.

38

"No! Not in the house!"
Said the fish in the pot.
"They should not fly kites
In a house! They should not.
Oh, the things they will bump!
Oh, the things they will hit!
Oh, I do not like it!
Not one little bit!"

Then Sally and I

Saw them run down the hall.

We saw those two Things

Bump their kites on the wall!

Bump! Thump! Thump! Bump!

Down the wall in the hall.

Thing Two and Thing One!

They ran up! They ran down!

On the string of one kite

We saw Mother's new gown!

Her gown with the dots

That are pink, white and red.

Then we saw one kite bump

On the head of her bed!

42

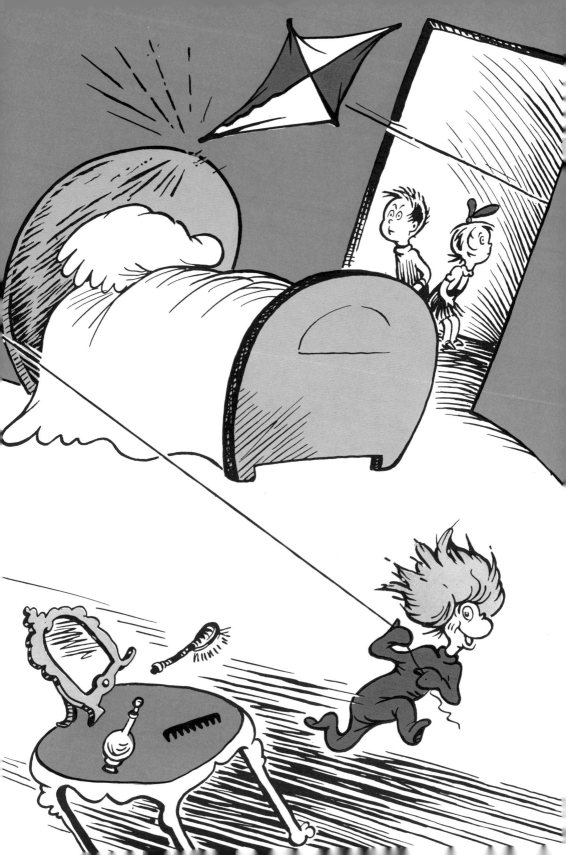

Then those Things ran about

With big bumps, jumps and kicks

And with hops and big thumps

And all kinds of bad tricks.

And I said,

"I do NOT like the way that they play!

If Mother could see this,

Oh, what would she say!"

45

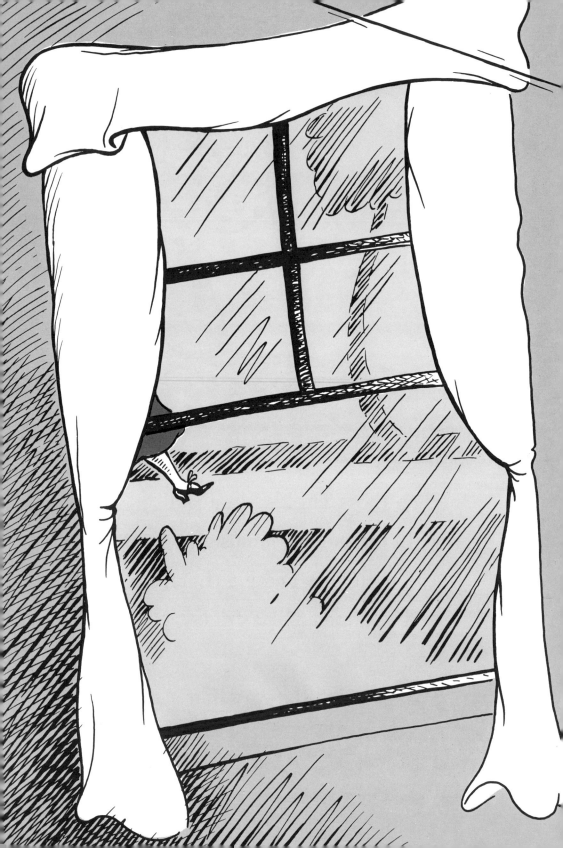

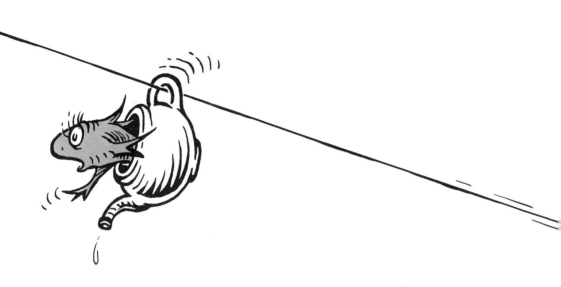

Then our fish said, "Look! Look!"

And our fish shook with fear.

"Your mother is on her way home!

Do you hear?

Oh, what will she do to us?

What will she say?

Oh, she will not like it

To find us this way!"

47

"So, DO something! Fast!" said the fish.

"Do you hear!

I saw her. Your mother!

Your mother is near!

So, as fast as you can,

Think of something to do!

You will have to get rid of

Thing One and Thing Two!"

So, as fast as I could,

I went after my net.

And I said, "With my net

I can get them I bet.

I bet, with my net,

I can get those Things yet!"

Then I let down my net.

It came down with a PLOP!

And I had them! At last!

Those two Things had to stop.

Then I said to the cat,

"Now you do as I say.

You pack up those Things

And you take them away!"

"Oh dear!" said the cat.

"You did not like our game . . .

Oh dear.

What a shame!

What a shame!

What a shame!"

53

Then he shut up the Things

In the box with the hook.

And the cat went away

With a sad kind of look.

"That is good," said the fish.

"He has gone away. Yes.

But your mother will come.

She will find this big mess!

And this mess is so big

And so deep and so tall,

We can not pick it up.

There is no way at all!"

55

And THEN!

Who was back in the house?

Why, the cat!

"Have no fear of this mess,"

Said the Cat in the Hat.

"I always pick up all my playthings

And so . . .

I will show you another

Good trick that I know!"

57

Then we saw him pick up

All the things that were down.

He picked up the cake,

And the rake, and the gown,

And the milk, and the strings,

And the books, and the dish,

And the fan, and the cup,

And the ship, and the fish.

And he put them away.

Then he said, "That is that."

And then he was gone

With a tip of his hat.

Then our mother came in
And she said to us two,
"Did you have any fun?
Tell me. What did you do?"

And Sally and I did not know
What to say.
Should we tell her
The things that went on there that day?

Should we tell her about it?

Now, what SHOULD we do?

Well . . .

What would YOU do

If your mother asked YOU?

61

Dr.Seuss™

The more that you **read**,
the more things **you** will know.
The more that you **learn**,
the **more** places you'll go!

– I Can Read With My Eyes Shut!

With over **35 paperbacks to collect** there's a book for all ages and reading abilities, and now there's never been a better time to have **fun** with **Dr.Seuss!** Simply collect 5 tokens from the back of each Dr.Seuss book and send in for your

FREE Dr.Seuss poster

(rrp £3.99)

Send your 5 tokens and a completed voucher to:

Dr. Seuss poster offer, PO Box 142, Horsham, UK, RH13 5FJ (UK residents only)

Title: Mr ☐ Mrs ☐ Miss ☐ Ms ☐

First Name:_____ Surname:_____

Address:_____

Post Code:_____ E-Mail Address:_____

Date of Birth:_____ Signature of parent/guardian:_____

TICK HERE IF YOU DO NOT WISH TO RECEIVE FURTHER INFORMATION ABOUT CHILDREN'S BOOKS ☐

TERMS AND CONDITIONS: Proof of sending cannot be considered proof of receipt. Not redeemable for cash.
Please allow 28 days for delivery. Photocopied tokens not accepted. Offer open to UK only.

Read them **together**, read them **alone**, read them **aloud** and make **reading fun!**
With over **30 wacky** stories to choose from, now it's **easier** than **ever** to find the
right **Dr. Seuss** books for your child – just let the **back cover colour** guide you!

Blue back books
for sharing with your child

Dr. Seuss' ABC
The Foot Book
Hop on Pop
Mr. Brown Can Moo! Can You?
One Fish, Two Fish, Red Fish, Blue Fish
There's a Wocket in my Pocket!

Green back books
for children just beginning to read on their own

And to Think That I Saw It on Mulberry Street
The Cat in the Hat
The Cat in the Hat Comes Back
Fox in Socks
Green Eggs and Ham
I Can Read With My Eyes Shut!
I Wish That I Had Duck Feet
Marvin K. Mooney Will You Please Go Now!
Oh, Say Can You Say?
Oh, the Thinks You Can Think!
Ten Apples Up on Top
Wacky Wednesday
Hunches in Bunches
Happy Birthday to YOU

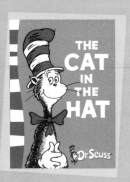

Yellow back books
for fluent readers to enjoy

Daisy-Head Mayzie
Did I Ever Tell You How Lucky You Are?
Dr. Seuss' Sleep Book
Horton Hatches the Egg
Horton Hears a Who!
How the Grinch Stole Christmas!
If I Ran the Circus
If I Ran the Zoo
I Had Trouble in Getting to Solla Sollew
The Lorax
Oh, the Places You'll Go!
On Beyond Zebra
Scrambled Eggs Super!
The Sneetches and other stories
Thidwick the Big-Hearted Moose
Yertle the Turtle and other stories

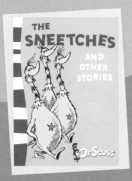

So . . .
be your name Buxbaum or Bixby or Bray
or Mordecai Ali Van Allen O'Shea,
you're off to Great Places!
Today is your day!
Your mountain is waiting.
So . . . *get on your way!*

And will you succeed?
Yes! You will, indeed!
(98 and ¾ per cent guaranteed.)

KID, YOU'LL MOVE MOUNTAINS!

You'll get mixed up, of course,
as you already know.
You'll get mixed up
with many strange birds as you go.
So be sure when you step.
Step with care and great tact
and remember that Life's
a Great Balancing Act.
Just never forget to be dexterous and deft.
And *never* mix up your right foot with your left.

On and on you will hike.
And I know you'll hike far
and face up to your problems
whatever they are.

But on you will go
though the weather be foul.
On you will go
though your enemies prowl.
On you will go
though the Hakken-Kraks howl.
Onward up many
a frightening creek,
though your arms may get sore
and your sneakers may leak.

And when you're alone, there's a very good chance
you'll meet things that scare you right out of your pants.
There are some, down the road between hither and yon,
that can scare you so much you won't want to go on.

All Alone!
Whether you like it or not,
Alone will be something
you'll be quite a lot.

Except when they *don't*.
Because, sometimes, they *won't*.

I'm afraid that *some* times
you'll play lonely games too.
Games you can't win
'cause you'll play against you.

Oh, the places you'll go! There is fun to be done!
There are points to be scored. There are games to be won.
And the magical things you can do with that ball
will make you the winning-est winner of all.
Fame! You'll be famous as famous can be,
with the whole wide world watching you win on TV.

With banner flip-flapping,
once more you'll ride high!
Ready for anything under the sky.
Ready because you're that kind of a guy!

NO!
That's not for you!

Somehow you'll escape
all that waiting and staying.
You'll find the bright places
where Boom Bands are playing.

Waiting for the fish to bite
or waiting for wind to fly a kite
or waiting around for Friday night
or waiting, perhaps, for their Uncle Jake
or a pot to boil, or a Better Break
or a string of pearls, or a pair of pants
or a wig with curls, or Another Chance.
Everyone is just waiting.

. . . for people just waiting.
    Waiting for a train to go
    or a bus to come, or a plane to go
    or the mail to come, or the rain to go
    or the phone to ring, or the snow to snow
    or waiting around for a Yes or No
    or waiting for their hair to grow.
    Everyone is just waiting.

You can get so confused
that you'll start in to race
down long wiggled roads at a break-necking pace
and grind on for miles across weirdish wild space,
headed, I fear, toward a most useless place.

The Waiting Place . . .

And *IF* you go in, should you turn left or right . . .
or right–and–three–quarters? Or, maybe, not quite?
Or go around back and sneak in from behind?
Simple it's not, I'm afraid you will find,
for a mind–maker–upper to make up his mind.

You will come to a place where the streets are not marked.
Some windows are lighted. But mostly they're darked.
A place you could sprain both your elbow and chin!
Do you dare to stay out? Do you dare to go in?
How much can you lose? How much can you win?

And when you're in a Slump,
you're not in for much fun.
Un-slumping yourself
is not easily done.

You'll come down from the Lurch
with an unpleasant bump.
And the chances are, then,
that you'll be in a Slump.

I'm sorry to say so
but, sadly, it's true
that Bang-ups
and Hang-ups
can happen to you.

You can get all hung up
in a prickle-ly perch.
And your gang will fly on.
You'll be left in a Lurch.

Except when you *don't*.
Because, sometimes, you *won't*.

You won't lag behind, because you'll have the speed.
You'll pass the whole gang and you'll soon take the lead.
Wherever you fly, you'll be best of the best.
Wherever you go, you will top all the rest.

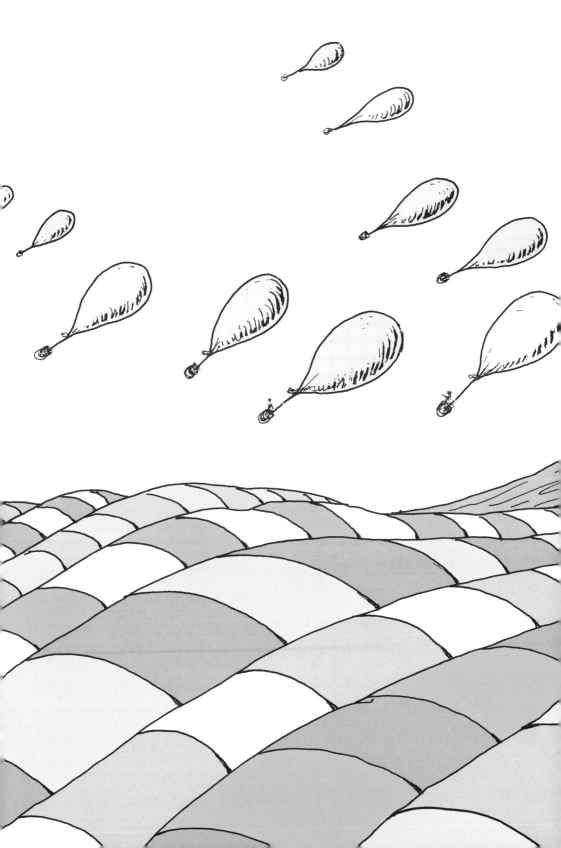

You'll be on your way up!
You'll be seeing great sights!
You'll join the high fliers
who soar to high heights.

OH!
THE PLACES YOU'LL GO!

And when things start to happen,
don't worry. Don't stew.
Just go right along.
You'll start happening too.

Out there things can happen
and frequently do
to people as brainy
and footsy as you.

It's opener there
in the wide open air.

And you may not find *any*
you'll want to go down.
In that case, of course,
you'll head straight out of town.

You'll look up and down streets. Look 'em over with care.
About some you will say, "I don't choose to go there."
With your head full of brains and your shoes full of feet,
you're too smart to go down any not-so-good street.

You have brains in your head.
You have feet in your shoes.
You can steer yourself
any direction you choose.
You're on your own. And you know what you know.
And *YOU* are the guy who'll decide where to go.

Congratulations!
Today is your day.
You're off to Great Places!
You're off and away!

Oh, the Places You'll Go!

By Dr. Seuss

"Nothing," I said, growing red as a beet,
"But a plain horse and wagon on Mulberry Street."

But Dad said quite calmly,
"Just draw up your stool
And tell me the sights
On the way home from school."

There was so much to tell, I JUST COULDN'T BEGIN!
Dad looked at me sharply and pulled at his chin.
He frowned at me sternly from there in his seat,
"Was there nothing to look at . . . no people to greet?
Did *nothing* excite you or make your heart beat?"

I swung round the corner
And dashed through the gate,
I ran up the steps
And I felt simply GREAT!

FOR I HAD A STORY THAT **NO ONE** COULD BEAT!
AND TO THINK THAT I SAW IT ON MULBERRY STREET!

A ten-foot beard
That needs a comb. . . .

No time for more,
I'm almost home.

. . . A Chinaman
Who eats with sticks. . . .

A big Magician
Doing tricks . . .

And that makes a story that's really not bad!
But it still could be better. Suppose that I add . . . .

With a roar of its motor an aeroplane appears
And dumps out confetti while everyone cheers.

The Mayor is there
And the Aldermen too,
All waving big banners
Of red, white and blue.

And that is a story that NO ONE can beat
When I say that I saw it on Mulberry Street!

The Mayor is there
And he thinks it is grand,
And he raises his hat
As they dash by the stand.

They'll never crash now. They'll race at top speed
With Sergeant Mulvaney, himself, in the lead.

It takes Police to do the trick,
To guide them through where traffic's thick—
It takes Police to do the trick.

Unless there's something I can fix up,
There'll be an *awful* traffic mix-up!

But now what worries me is this . .
Mulberry Street runs into Bliss,

But now is it fair? Is it fair what I've done?
I'll bet those wagons weigh more than a ton.
That's really too heavy a load for *one* beast;
I'll give him some helpers. He needs two, at least.

A band that's so good should have someone to hear it,
But it's going so fast that it's hard to keep near it.
I'll put on a trailer! I know they won't mind
If a man sits and listens while hitched on behind.

But he'd look simply grand
With a great big brass band!

But now I don't know . . .
It still doesn't seem right.

An elephant pulling a thing that's so light
Would whip it around in the air like a kite.

I'll pick one with plenty of power and size,
A blue one with plenty of fun in his eyes.
And then, just to give him a little more tone,
Have a Rajah, with rubies, perched high on a throne.

Say! That makes a story that *no one* can beat,
When I say that I saw it on Mulberry Street.

Hmmmm . . . A reindeer and sleigh . .

Say—*any*one could think of *that*,
Jack or Fred or Joe or Nat—
Say, even Jane could think of *that*.

But it isn't too late to make one little change.
A sleigh and an ELEPHANT! *There's* something strange!

He'd be much happier, instead,
If he could pull a fancy sled.

Hold on a minute!
There's something wrong!

A reindeer hates the way it feels
To pull a thing that runs on wheels.

And he'd look mighty smart
On old Mulberry Street.

No, it won't do at all . . .
A zebra's too small.

A reindeer is better;
He's fast and he's fleet,

Yes, the zebra is fine,
But I think it's a shame,
Such a marvellous beast
With a cart that's so tame.
The story would really be better to hear
If the driver I saw were a charioteer.
A gold and blue chariot's *something* to meet,
Rumbling like thunder down Mulberry Street!

That's nothing to tell of,
That won't do, of course . . .
Just a broken-down wagon
That's drawn by a horse.

That *can't* be my story. That's only a *start*.
I'll say that a ZEBRA was pulling that cart!
And that is a story that no one can beat,
When I say that I saw it on Mulberry Street.

All the long way to school
And all the way back,
I've looked and I've looked
And I've kept careful track,
But all that I've noticed,
Except my own feet,
Was a horse and a wagon
On Mulberry Street.

WHEN I leave home to walk to school,
Dad always says to me,
"Marco, keep your eyelids up
And see what you can see."

But when I tell him where I've been
And what I think I've seen,
He looks at me and sternly says,
"Your eyesight's much too keen.

"Stop telling such outlandish tales.
Stop turning minnows into whales."

Now, what can I say
When I get home today?

For Helen McC.
Mother of the One and Original Marco

AND TO THINK THAT I SAW IT ON MULBERRY STREET

By Dr. Seuss

Today is gone. Today was fun.
Tomorrow is another one.
Every day,
from here to there,
funny things are everywhere.

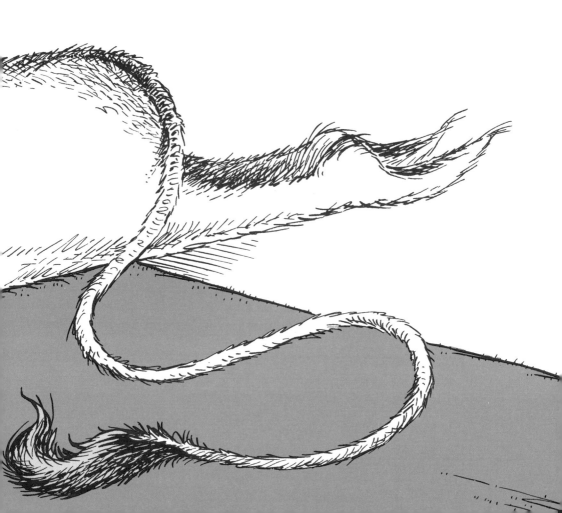

And now
good night.
It is time to sleep.
So we will sleep
with our pet Zeep.

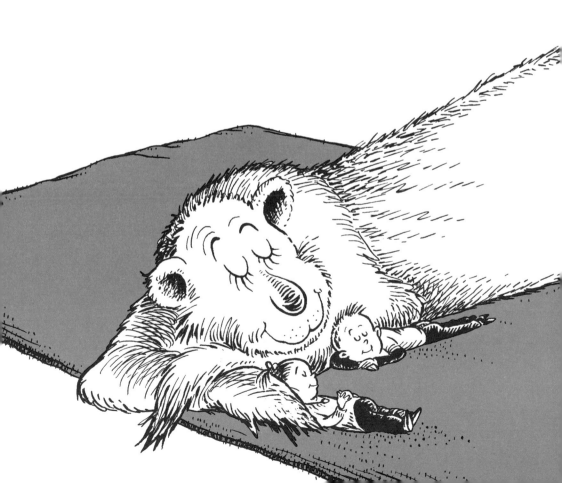

Look what we found

in the park

in the dark.

We will take him home.

We will call him Clark.

He will live at our house.

He will grow and grow.

Will our mother like this?

We don't know.

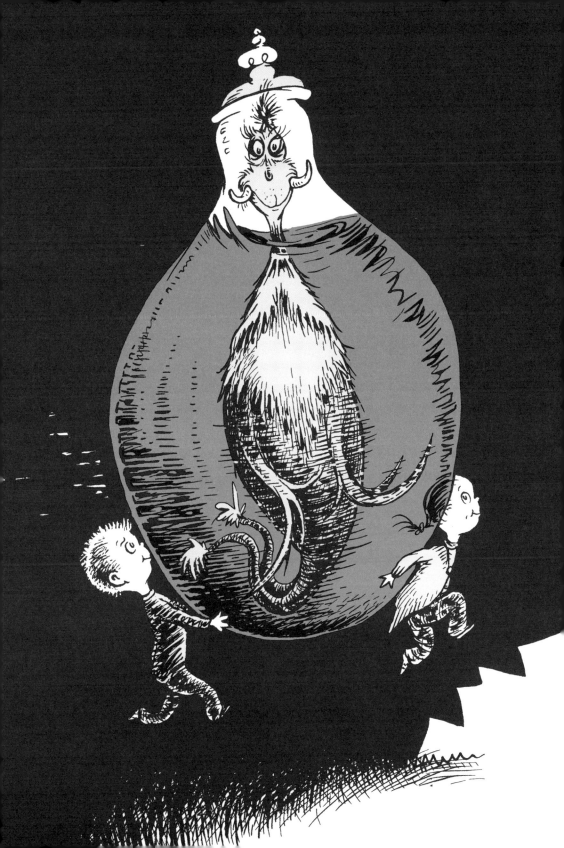

At our house
we play out back.
We play a game
called Ring the Gack.

Would you like to play this game?
Come down!
We have the only
Gack in town.

When I wish to make a wish
I wave my hand with a big swish swish.
Then I say, "I wish for fish!"
And I get fish right on my dish.

So . . . .

if you wish to wish a wish,

you may swish for fish

with my Ish wish dish.

Who am I?

My name is Ish.

On my hand I have a dish.

I have this dish
to help me wish.

From near to far
from here to there,
funny things are everywhere.

These yellow pets
are called the Zeds.
They have one hair
up on their heads.
Their hair grows fast . . .
so fast, they say,
they need a hair cut
every day.

Oh, no.

I can not hear your call.

I can not hear your call at all.

This is not good

and I know why.

A mouse has cut the wire.

Good-bye!

Hello!
Hello!
Are you there?
Hello!
I called you up
to say hello.
I said hello.
Can you hear me, Joe?

Did you ever milk
this kind of cow?
Well, we can do it.
We know how.

If you never did,
you should.
These things are fun
and fun is good.

Did you ever
fly a kite
in bed?

Did you ever walk
with ten cats
on your head?

Who is this pet?
Say!
He is wet.

You never yet
met a pet,
I bet,
as wet as they let
this wet pet get.

Brush! Brush!
Brush! Brush!

Comb! Comb!
Comb! Comb!

Blue hair
is fun
to brush and comb.

All girls who like
to brush and comb
should have a pet
like this at home.

I like to hop
all day and night
from right to left
and left to right.

Why do I like to
hop, hop, hop?
I do not know.
Go ask your Pop.

Hop! Hop! Hop!
I am a Yop.
All I like to do is hop
from finger top
to finger top.

I hop from left to right
and then . . .
Hop! Hop!
I hop right back again.

He likes to drink, and drink, and drink.
The thing he likes to drink
is ink.
The ink he likes to drink is pink.
He likes to wink and drink pink ink.

SO . . .

if you have a lot of ink,
then you should get
a Yink, I think.

This one,
I think,
is called
a Yink.

He likes to wink,

he likes to drink.

It is fun to sing
if you sing with a Ying.
My Ying can sing
like anything.

I sing high
and my Ying sings low,
and we are not too bad,
you know.

In yellow socks

I box my Gox.

I box in yellow

Gox box socks.

I like to box.

How I like to box!

So, every day,

I box a Gox.

At our house

we open cans.

We have to open

many cans.

And that is why

we have a Zans.

A Zans for cans

is very good.

Have you a Zans for cans?

You should.

I do not like
this one so well.
All he does
is yell, yell, yell.
I will not have this one about.
When he comes in
I put him out.

This one is
quiet as a mouse.
I like to have him
in the house.

By the light of the moon,
by the light of a star,
they walked all night
from near to far.

I would never walk.
I would take a car.

The moon was out
and we saw some sheep.
We saw some sheep
take a walk in their sleep.

We saw him sit
and try to cook.
He took a look
at the book on the hook.

But a Nook can't read,
so a Nook can't cook.
SO . . .
what good to a Nook
is a hook cook book?

We took a look.

We saw a Nook.

On his head

he had a hook.

On his hook

he had a book.

On his book

was "How to Cook."

My shoe is off.
My foot is cold.

I have a bird
I like to hold.

My hat is old.
My teeth are gold.

And now
my story
is all told.

My hat is old.
My teeth are gold.

I have a bird
I like to hold.

My shoe is off.
My foot is cold.

Say, look!

A bird was in your ear.

But he is out. So have no fear.

Again your ear can hear, my dear.

Oh, dear! Oh, dear!

I can not hear.

Will you please

come over near?

Will you please look in my ear?

There must be something there, I fear.

I do not like
this bed at all.
A lot of things
have come to call.
A cow, a dog, a cat, a mouse.
Oh! what a bed! Oh! what a house!

Hello there, Ned.
How do you do?
Tell me, tell me
what is new?
How are things
in your little bed?
What is new?
Please tell me, Ned.

We like our Mike
and this is why:
Mike does all the work
when the hills get high.

We like our bike.
It is made for three.
Our Mike
sits up in back,
you see.

And when I pull them in,
Oh, dear!
My head sticks out of bed
up here!

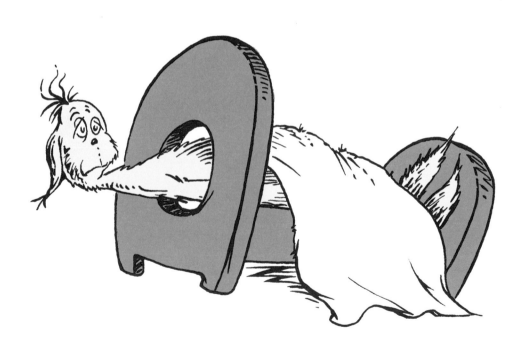

Who am I?
My name is Ned.
I do not like
my little bed.

    This is no good.
    This is not right.
    My feet stick out
    of bed all night.

But

we know a man

called Mr. Gump.

Mr. Gump has a seven hump Wump.

So . . .

if you like to go Bump! Bump!

just jump on the hump of the Wump of Gump.

Bump!

Bump!

Bump!

Did you ever ride a Wump?

We have a Wump

with just one hump.

Say!

Look at his fingers!

One, two, three . . .

How many fingers

do I see?

One, two, three, four,

five, six, seven,

eight, nine, ten.

He has eleven!

Eleven!

This is something new.

I wish I had

eleven, too!

Some are high.

And some are low.

Not one of them
is like another.
Don't ask us why.
Go ask your mother.

We see them come.

We see them go.

Some are fast.

And some are slow.

Where do they come from? I can't say.

But I bet they have come

a long, long way.

Some have two feet
and some have four.
Some have six feet
and some have more.

Oh me! Oh my!
Oh me! Oh my!
What a lot
of funny things go by.

Here are some
who like to run.
They run for fun
in the hot, hot sun.

From there to here,
from here to there,
funny things
are everywhere.

Some are thin.

And some are fat.
The fat one has
a yellow hat.

And some are very, very bad.

Why are they
sad and glad and bad?
I do not know.
Go ask your dad.

Yes. Some are red. And some are blue.
Some are old. And some are new.

Some are sad.

And some are glad.

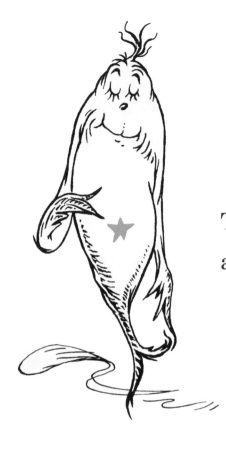

This one has
a little star.

This one has a little car.
Say! what a lot
of fish there are.

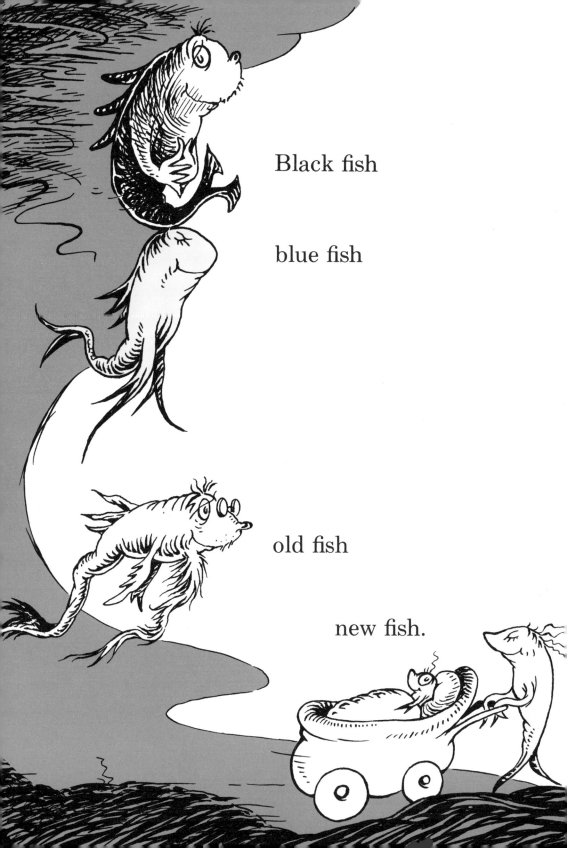

Black fish

blue fish

old fish

new fish.

One fish

two fish

red fish

blue fish.

From there to here,
from here to there,
funny things
are everywhere.

One fish
two fish
red fish
blue fish

By Dr. Seuss

Time To Read with Dr. Seuss
™ & © Dr. Seuss Enterprises, L.P. 2006
All rights reserved

An omnibus edition adapted from
One Fish, Two Fish, Red Fish, Blue Fish,
And To Think That I Saw It On Mulberry Street
and *Oh, The Places You'll Go*
Published by HarperCollins*Children's Books*,
77-85 Fulham Palace Road, London W6 8JB

Visit our website at:
www.harpercollinschildrensbooks.co.uk

1 3 5 7 9 10 8 6 4 2

ISBN 0-00-722850-3
ISBN-13: 978-0-00-722850-8

One Fish, Two Fish, Red Fish, Blue Fish © 1960, 1988
by Dr. Seuss Enterprises, L.P. All rights reserved.
Published by arrangement with Random House Inc., New York,
USA. First published in the UK in 1960.
And To Think That I Saw It On Mulberry Street © 1937, 1964
by Dr. Seuss Enterprises, L.P. All rights reserved.
Published by arrangement with Random House Inc., New York,
USA. First published in the UK in 1971.
Oh, The Places You'll Go © 1990
by Dr. Seuss Enterprises, L.P. All rights reserved.
Published by arrangement with Random House Inc., New York,
USA. First published in the UK in 1990

Printed and bound in Hong Kong

TIME TO READ
WITH
Dr. Seuss

ONE FISH, TWO FISH, RED FISH, BLUE FISH

AND TO THINK THAT I SAW
IT ON MULBERRY STREET

OH, THE PLACES YOU'LL GO!

HarperCollins *Children's Books*